The Poodle Who Barked at the Wind

Charlotte Zolotow

ILLUSTRATIONS BY
Valerie Coursen

HENRY HOLT AND COMPANY
NEW YORK

Henry Holt and Company, LLC
Publishers since 1866
115 West 18th Street, New York, New York 10011
www.henryholt.com

Henry Holt is a registered trademark of Henry Holt and Company, LLC
Text copyright © 1964 by Charlotte Zolotow
Illustrations copyright © 2002 by Valerie Coursen
Distributed in Canada by H. B. Fenn and Company Ltd.

Library of Congress Cataloging-in-Publication Data
Zolotow, Charlotte. The poodle who barked at the wind / by Charlotte Zolotow;
illustrations by Valerie Coursen.
Summary: A family's noisy little poodle barks at everything, disturbing the father,
until the day everyone else goes out and the father and poodle are left alone together.
[1. Dogs—Fiction.] I. Coursen, Valerie, ill. II. Title.
PZ7.Z77 Po 2002   [E]—dc21   2001006290   ISBN 0-8050-6306-4
Published in 1964 by Lothrop, Lee & Shepard with illustrations by Roger Duvoisin.
Published in 1987 by Harper & Row with illustrations by June Otani.
First Henry Holt Edition—2002 / Designed by Donna Mark
Printed in the United States of America on acid-free paper. ∞

1 3 5 7 9 10 8 6 4 2

The artist used mixed-media collage to create
the illustrations for this book.

For Peter Hays with love
—C. Z.

For my children, Chad, Sam, and Amelia
—V. C.

Once there was a family with a little black poodle. She was a noisy little poodle who barked at everything.

She barked at the garbagemen.

She barked at the postman.

She barked at the milkman.

She barked at the telephone when it rang and the wind when it blew and the rain when it rained.

The children in the family would stop what they were doing to see why the little poodle was barking.

The mother would look up from her work to find out why the little poodle was barking.

But the father of the family was a writer and worked at home. The little poodle's barking made him forget what he wanted to write.

"Oh, why do you bark so much?" he would ask the little black poodle. But she would just sit down in front of him.

Every time the phone rang, the little poodle barked.

Every time the doorbell rang, the little poodle raced to it, barking loudly.

Every time the postman came, the little poodle barked.

The father would come down
for his letters and look at the
little poodle.

"Why do you bark so much?"
he'd say, and the little poodle would
sit down in front of him and wag her
tail as though the father had patted her
on the head.

Sometimes the mother went out.
Sometimes the little boy went out.
Sometimes the little girl went out.
But one day they all went out together.
They left the little poodle's food in her
dish and her water in her bowl.

"Take care of her," the children
said when they kissed their father
good-bye. "She'll be lonely."

"So will I," said the father.
"We'll be back for dinner,"
the mother said quickly,
"and the house will be nice
and quiet for you today."

"QUIET!" said the father. "With that poodle here?"

He looked at the poodle, and the little poodle wagged her tail at him. The father climbed upstairs to his study and closed the door with a bang.

He worked at his typewriter all morning.

But the poodle didn't know the mother and the children were coming back for dinner. She didn't understand their leaving and now she felt all alone. She couldn't eat her food. She couldn't drink her water.

When the father opened his study door and started downstairs for lunch, he stumbled over something soft that had been pressed up against his door.

It was the little black poodle.

She scrambled to her feet, but she didn't bark.

She walked downstairs with him, rubbing against his ankle as though she were his shadow.

While he ate lunch, she went under the table and put her head on his foot.

"Go eat your lunch," the father said. But the little poodle couldn't eat.

The postman brought the mail.

But the little poodle didn't bark.

The milkman brought the milk.

But the little poodle didn't bark.

The wind blew outside, and the little poodle

just lay on the father's foot.

The telephone rang, and when the father got up to answer it the little poodle trotted along by his side without making a sound.

"Why don't you bark?" the father said. But the little poodle only put her head into the curve of his hand for him to pat her.

The father went back upstairs to work, and like a small black shadow at his ankle went the little poodle, almost as though she were attached to him.

He closed the door to his study, but in a minute he opened it again. He almost tripped over something warm and black pressed up against the door.

"Oh, come in then," the father said, and the little poodle came in and went under the father's desk and lay there on his foot.

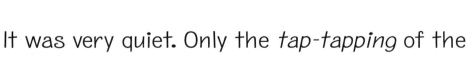

It was very quiet. Only the *tap-tapping* of the typewriter filled the room.

Outside, soft little pats of rain fell against the window, and the wind shook the house. But the little poodle lay there on the father's foot. When the father stopped typing to think, it was absolutely quiet except for the wind and the rain.

The father looked down.

"Why don't you bark?" he asked the poodle, but she just looked up at him without making a sound.

Late in the afternoon she jumped up suddenly and ran from the desk to the door of the father's study.

Her tail waved back and forth like a black-handled mop.

The father opened the door, and the little poodle raced down the stairs.

Her family was home! The awful feeling of the
empty house was gone. She ran back and forth
from the mother to the children, barking happily.

She ran to her bowl and swallowed the whole dish of food that had been there all day. She drank her water noisily, and wagging her tail she ran from the windows to the doors, barking and barking, though there was nothing outside but the wind.

Upstairs the father heard her and smiled to himself.

She's happy again, he thought. She's taking care of things.

Never again did he say, "Why do you bark
so much?" He knew the little poodle's barking
meant that his wife and children were in the
house, and the little poodle was feeling protective
and brave and bold, warning them about bells and
people and the rain and the wind.

The End!